Little Wombat was looking for apples.
"Hello," said a funny squeaky voice.
Wombat spun around.
"Hello! I'm Wombat, who are you?"
"I'm Platypus," said a funny fuzzy face.

Then, with a funny shuffly walk, Platypus waddled to the pond and disappeared.

Swim, Little Wombat, Swim!

Charles Fuge

WALKER BOOKS
AND SUBSIDIARIES

LONDON • BOSTON • SYDNEY • AUCKLAND

"PLA-TY-PUS!" Little Wombat giggled.
"PLA-TY-PUS!"

He tried to waddle too. He giggled and
waddled, shuffled and chuckled nearer and
nearer to the water's edge . . .

KER-SPLASH!

Little Wombat sank like a stone.

In a flash, Platypus
darted towards him.

Before he knew it, Wombat
was at the surface . . .

and safely out of the water.
"Thank you, Platypus," he spluttered.
He wished he hadn't laughed at his new friend.
"How did you learn to swim like that?"
"It's easy!" Platypus smiled.
"I'll teach you!"

First, Little Wombat had to hold onto the edge and kick his legs as hard as he could.

Then he used a log as a float, and he splashed all around the pond.

He splashed and kicked until
he was worn out.
"Time for lunch!" said Platypus.

Little Wombat munched on juicy red apples and Platypus munched on a handful of shrimps.
"Never swim on a full tummy," said Platypus. So they snoozed in the shade for an hour.

That afternoon, Little Wombat learned to paddle like a dog . . .

and dive like a frog!

Then, through all the splashing,
Little Wombat heard his
name being called.

Rabbit and Koala had come to see
what he had been doing all day.
Little Wombat beamed.
"PLATYPUS taught me to swim!
Come on, Platypus, let's have a race."

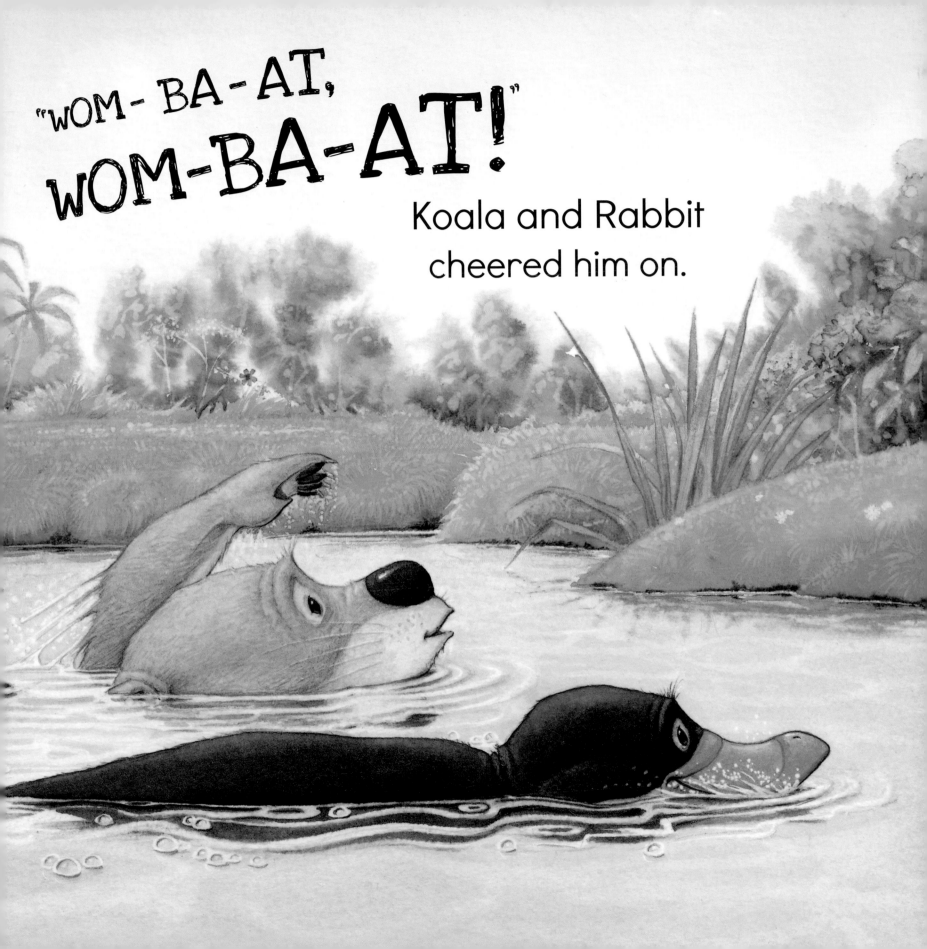

"WOM-BA-AT, WOM-BA-AT!"

Koala and Rabbit cheered him on.

"No … not Wombat …" Little Wombat grinned at his new friend.

"WOM-BATYPUS!"

For Oliver Churchill Fuge
born 2 December, 2004
C.F.

This edition published 2021 by Walker Books Ltd
87 Vauxhall Walk, London SE11 5HJ

2 4 6 8 10 9 7 5 3 1

First published 2005 by Gullane Children's Books

This book has been typeset in Didact Gothic and Love Ya Like A Sister

Printed in China

British Library Cataloguing in Publication Data: a catalogue record for this book
is available from the British Library

ISBN 978-1-5295-0627-3

www.walker.co.uk